Abracadabra!

YiKES!

It's Alive!

Anything can happen when you wave your magic wand!

Join the Abracadabra Club in all their Magical Mysteries.

#1: **POOF!** Rabbits Everywhere!

#2: **Boo!** Ghosts in the School!

#3: **PRESTO!** Magic Treasure!

#4: **YEEPS!** Secret in the Statue!

#5: **ZAP!** Science Fair Surprise!

#6: **YiKES!** It's Alive!

Abracadabra!

YIKES!

It's Alive!

By Peter Lerangis
Illustrated by Jim Talbot

A
LITTLE APPLE
PAPERBACK

SCHOLASTIC INC.
New York Toronto London Auckland Sydney
Mexico City New Delhi Hong Kong Buenos Aires

For the Brewster boys,
Jack and Ben

ISBN 0-439-38937-2

12 11 10 9 8 7 6 5 4 3 2 1   3 4 5 6 7 8/0
                                           40
Printed in the U.S.A.
First Scholastic printing, March 2003

Contents

1

We're Not in Rebus Anymore

"Oh!" gasped Jessica Frimmel.

"EEEEEEE!" screamed her little brother, Noah.

"Ahhh," said her teacher, Mr. Beamish.

"Blzrp," gulped Andrew Flingus, nearly choking on a tuna-marshmallow sandwich.

From high above, a scary skeleton stared down. Its claws were bent. Its teeth were long and sharp.

"STAND BACK, O GREAT AND HORRIBLE BEAST!" shouted Max Bleeker, whooshing his big black cape. "OR I SHALL CAST A SPELL AND TURN YOUR BONES INTO RUST!"

"You mean *dust*," hissed Selena Cruz. "Not *rust*!"

Max wore a black cape and a top hat every day. He also mixed up his words when he was excited.

On that day, everyone was excited. The Rebus Elementary School science fair team was in New York City! They had won first prize in the town science fair. And that meant a trip to the American Museum of Natural History.

Wherever Max went, he tried to do magic. He loved magic even more than he loved dinosaurs. He, Selena, and Jessica were members of the Abracadabra Club, Rebus Elementary School's only club for magicians and detectives.

So was their friend Quincy Norton. Quincy, as usual, had his nose in a book. It was called *Everything About New York*.

"Did you know that the American Museum of Natural History opened in 1877?" said Quincy. "It is four stories high and four blocks long. It is connected to the subway, and it is only two hundred seventeen and a half miles from Rebus."

Jessica peeked over his shoulder. "*Rebus* is in that book?"

"No," said Quincy. "I measured the distance on a map."

Quincy was the smartest kid in the fourth grade. He loved numbers. He knew that there were eleven third graders, seventeen fourth graders, fifteen fifth graders, six parents, and five teachers on the trip to New York. (Not to mention one little brother, Noah, who came along because Jessica's dad was one of the parent chaperones.)

Quincy also knew the length, weight, and name of every dinosaur in the room. He knew almost as much as Ms. Mandible, the museum lady.

"This skeleton belonged to a *Tyrannosaurus*," said Ms. Mandible. "Can you tell us how old this dinosaur is, Quincy?"

"It's from the Cretaceous Era, to be exact," said Quincy, "so it's been dead for at least sixty-five million years."

"Then how come it doesn't smell?" asked Andrew. "Dead hamsters smell after two days."

Selena made a sour face. "So do boys who eat tuna-marshmallow sandwiches."

"The dinosaurs ruled the earth for more than one hundred seventy million years — a thousand times longer than humans have," said Ms. Mandible. "Then, suddenly — *poof*! They were gone. The *Tyrannosaurus*, the *Triceratops* — they all died in the Great Extinction."

"I told you they stinked!" Andrew said.

"Stank," Jessica corrected him.

"No one knows why they all died," Ms. Mandible went on. "Was it because a meteor hit the earth? Did dust from volcanoes block the sun? Did smaller creatures eat the dinosaur eggs?"

She pointed to an exhibit behind glass. It showed a dried, cracked land. Ugly little animals were eating the bodies of dead dinosaurs.

Mr. Yu, the art teacher, knelt by the glass. "Look at how real those stuffed creatures look. I wish I could make models like that."

"For millions of years, these little critters were dinosaur food," said Ms. Mandible. "But once the dinosaurs were gone, things changed. Big creatures were out. Little ones were in. They took over the world, because they were not being hunted anymore. And then, over millions more years, *they* became bigger! Some became horses, dogs, and elephants. Those with a certain kind of brain became . . . us. Human beings!"

Mr. Yu laughed. "Which means those critters are our great-great-great-great-great-great-great-great-great-great-great-great-great-grandparents! We're related!"

"Ew. I don't look like that," said Selena. She began brushing her hair, which always made her feel better.

"But there were small dinosaurs, too," said Quincy. "Didn't they live on — past the Great Extinction?"

"I'm afraid not," Ms. Mandible replied.

"Mammals ate them all," bragged Andrew. "GO MAMMALS!"

"In some places, there were no mammals to take over when dinosaurs became extinct," Ms. Mandible went on, leading everyone out of the room and down a set of stairs. "And in those places, some strange things happened."

On the third floor, she stopped by a glass cage that was labeled KOMODO DRAGONS. Inside, three giant, stuffed reptiles were being attacked by a warthog.

"These 'dragons' are really lizards," Ms. Mandible said. "They probably started out small, like regular lizards. But on the island of Komodo, there were no mammals to prey on them. So the *lizards* were the ones that evolved! You see, wherever the big creatures disappeared, the little ones grew."

"That's it!" Quincy exclaimed, looking up from his notepad. "That's where they could have lived!"

"Who?" asked Ms. Mandible.

"The little dinosaurs," Quincy answered. "What if they survived — in a place where there were no mammals? Like the island of Komodo. They could evolve there. They could grow. Maybe even become smart, like humans. Couldn't they?"

Ms. Mandible became quiet.

"Well," Quincy said, "couldn't they?"

Now everyone was staring at Ms. Mandible — teachers, kids, and parents.

A lock of silver-gray hair fell across her face. She looked left and right. "Follow me," she said in a low voice, hurrying down a long corridor.

"I don't like the sound of this," Selena said. "Where is she taking us?"

"Lunch, I hope," said Andrew.

"Come on!" urged Jessica, running ahead.

At the end of the corridor was a wooden door that said DO NOT ENTER: MUSEUM STAFF ONLY. "Come along, quickly!" Ms. Mandible whispered, opening the door.

Behind it was a big, empty room. In one corner stood a ladder, paint cans, and huge boxes. Ms. Mandible walked quickly to the opposite wall. There, a black curtain led to another room. She pulled the curtain aside and let everyone in.

Jessica squinted, but she could see nothing. The room was totally dark.

When the last person was in, Ms. Mandible let the curtain close.

"I'm scared," said Noah in a tiny voice.

"GREETINGS!" shouted a grinning dinosaur, jumping out from the dark.

2

Dino Island

"Yeeps!" yelled Quincy.

"Yuck!" said Selena.

"DON'T SCARE ME, BAD DINO-SAUR!" Noah ran to the creature and tried to bop it on the nose. But there was nothing there.

"I'm so sorry," Ms. Mandible said, flicking on a light. "Don't worry, this is only a hologram — a picture in three dimensions.

He looks like he's moving, but he's not. He's part of an exhibit that opens next month. I am giving you a sneak preview."

Jessica's heart was racing. The dinosaur looked so real. It had scaly greenish-yellow skin, pointed fingers, a big long head, and lizard eyes. But it stood on two legs, and it wore sandals, jeans, an orange T-shirt, and a New York Mets baseball cap.

"This dinosaur is a *Stenonychosaurus*," said Ms. Mandible. "Well, sort of. It's not what a Steno really looked like. It's what he *might* have looked like if the Steno were still alive. Some think the Steno is the *one* dinosaur that *could* have become smart like a human. You see, this dinosaur's brain was quite large."

"If he was so smart," said Andrew, "he would be a Red Sox fan."

Quincy sounded out the word as he wrote it: "Sten — no — niko — saurus . . ."

"He's cool," said Max.

"He's ugly," Selena grumbled, brushing her hair like crazy. "At least he is to me. But maybe that's just because I'm an artist. I like beautiful things."

"Besides," said Quincy, "if the Steno were alive now, it would look different. I mean, if those furry creatures evolved into us . . ."

"It might look human," Max said. "Or like an alien!"

"Or like you," said Andrew. "HAR! HAR! HAR!"

"As a matter of fact," said Ms. Mandible, "our museum is holding a 'Make a Steno' contest. We put ads in all the arts and science magazines. We're looking for the best model of what the Steno might look like today — if it were still alive."

"Could it be alive?" Max said. "That would be cool. Like, a whole colony of them. Living on an island. With an invisibility shield. And high-tech houses with huge computers!"

Jessica laughed. But the museum lady did not crack a smile. Instead, she shrugged her shoulders and nodded. "Well," she said. "I suppose anything is possible."

All day long, Ms. Mandible's words stuck in Jessica's mind. *Anything is possible.* Scientists and artists were working on these Steno models. They were the great brains of the world! Did they know something? Had they picked up a signal from a lost island? Were we humans in danger?

She was still thinking about it that night in her and Selena's hotel room. A big group had gathered there to tell ghost stories.

"Once upon a time," Selena said, holding a flashlight to her own face in the dark, "there was an island called Suber . . ."

"Suber?" Andrew Flingus blurted out. He was sitting on the floor, picking his ears.

"*Suber* is Rebus spelled backward," said Selena. "Now be quiet and don't spoil my story."

"I'm hungry," said Andrew.

"I have some fruit!" said Quincy. "But I'll only let you eat it under one condition. Everyone has to guess what kind of fruit is in this bag. I'll write the guesses on slips of paper, put them in Max's hat, and let Andrew pick one slip. If I guess which fruit is written on that slip, Andrew gets to eat it."

"*You guys!*" Selena complained.

"Apple!" cried Andrew.

"Apple . . ." Quincy said, writing on a piece of paper.

"Prune!" cried Bug Jones, one of the most annoying fourth graders.

"Banana!" said Charlene Crump.

"Chocolate!" Max called out. "Wait, I mean orange!"

Quincy wrote and wrote, then tore off each little slip of paper and put it in the hat. "Okay, Andrew, now pick a piece of paper — and don't tell me what it says!"

Andrew gritted his teeth and picked from the hat.

"I'll bet it says . . . this!" Quincy said, pulling a banana from the bag.

Andrew turned over the slip of paper he had picked. "It says *banana*! How did you do that?"

"Aw, I know that trick," said Bug. "*I* should be in the Abracadabra Club. See, what he did was —"

"A magician never reveals his tricks," said Quincy. "Now be quiet while Selena tells her ghost story."

"Ahem," said Selena, clearing her throat. "Lights, please."

Max put out the room lights, then sat down. He took a flashlight and shone it on the wall. In the light he made waving motions with his hands.

"*Max, what are you doing?*" Selena asked angrily.

"You said the story takes place on an *island,*" Max replied. "I'm making an ocean."

With a sigh, Selena went on. "In ancient times, ships would pass the island of Suber, but they all vanished — *poof* — without a trace! You see, some very strange creatures

17

lived on Suber. Dinosaurs, big and small. Dinosaurs who had survived the Great Extinction. Hungry *Tyrannosauruses*, peaceful *Brontosauruses*, flying *Pteranodons* . . ."

Max's hands made a tall blob, a long blob, and a flying blob.

"The big dinosaurs got very, very hungry," Selena went on, "and ate all the little ones. And so, over the years, the little ones all died out."

Max made his fingers walk, then slapped them away with his other hand.

Selena leaned forward. She lowered her voice to a whisper. "But secretly, a group of very small dinosaurs hid away. They knew the big ones would run out of food. So they waited. And waited. And finally the big dinosaurs became extinct. Over the ages, the little dinosaurs became smarter. Smarter than the most awesome computer. They could live with hardly any sleep or food. They paid no attention to the stupid creatures that ruled the rest of the world.

"But as time passed, they began to get worried about those creatures, the ones who were called humans. 'There are so many!' said the dinosaur leader, 'and not so many of us!' Well, the creatures knew they could wait no longer. So one day, they decided to leave the island of Suber! AND THEY AT-TACKED!"

In the glow of Max's flashlight, a shape appeared. But it wasn't one of Max's hands.

It had long, sharp teeth and pointy claws!

"AAAAAAAAAAGH!" screamed Erica.

Bug Jones was on the floor, laughing. In his right hand was a small plastic dinosaur. "Fooled you!"

Selena stood and turned on the lights.

"Give me that!" she scolded, grabbing the dinosaur from Bug. "Where did you find it?"

"Your backpack is unzipped," Bug said with a shrug. "It fell out."

Quincy gave Selena a funny look. "*You* bought a model lizard?"

"It must transform into a Barbie," said Max.

"You *broke* my zipper, Bug!" Selena shouted as she tried to close her backpack. "OUT! Everyone! Story time is over. Jessica and I must have our beauty sleep."

"You need it," said Andrew, stepping on his banana peel as he left. "HAR! HAR! HAR!"

As the kids all headed out, Selena turned to Jessica with a weary smile. "How was my story?"

"Great," said Jessica. "You're as good a storyteller as you are an artist!"

She was telling the truth. Sort of.

Selena was a good storyteller. But Jessica did not like the story.

Because she was worried that it might be true.

Face the Music

By Monday at lunchtime, Jessica was in a much better mood.

She was back in Rebus. She had lots of souvenirs. The Steno hologram was 217½ miles away.

And her teacher, Mr. Beamish, who was also in charge of the Abracadabra Club, had told her something exciting.

"Max, guess what?" she said, racing

into the cafeteria. Max was in a different class than Jessica, Selena, and Quincy. He hadn't heard the news.

"The Abracadabra Club has a job!" said Jessica.

Max was wearing a huge pair of glasses, with dinosaurs printed on them. "YES, A VERY TOUGH JOB! WE MUST SAVE THE SCHOOL FROM EVIL DINOSAURS DISGUISED AS HUMANS! AND THESE DINO-DETECTING GLASSES WILL DO THE TRICK! HARK — I SEE ONE NOW, AT THE HEAD OF THE LUNCH LINE!"

"That's just Andrew," Jessica said, quickly moving through the line. "And I don't mean *that* job — I mean a show! A real magic show! Mr. Beamish told us in class. Crump's Playworld is having a party for all of Rebus on Saturday. They first opened exactly seventy-five years ago — and they want us to do a show to celebrate the park's anniversary!"

Crump's Playworld was Rebus's big amusement park. It had a carousel, a Ferris wheel, a roller coaster, and go-carts.

Max grinned. "Really? For the whole village? We'll be famous!"

"If we can plan it in time," Jessica said, heading straight for Selena and Quincy's table. "Now come on, we have a million things to talk about."

But Bug Jones was already there, putting on a show of his own. "Now, watch this, it's the coolest trick ever," he said, holding up a strawberry jelly doughnut. "I put the doughnut on the table and cover it with a napkin . . ."

Quincy sighed. "Bug wants to join the Abracadabra Club."

"If he really wants to do magic," said

Selena, trying to close up her backpack, "he can fix this zipper he broke!"

"Go away, Bug," Jessica said. "We have business."

"Now you see it . . ." Bug slid the napkin along the table, toward him. When he got to the edge of the table, he lifted the napkin — and the doughnut was gone. "*Abracadabra!* I made the doughnut disappear! Isn't that cool?"

Jessica shook her head. "You did it all wrong. Let me show you how. Where's the doughnut?"

"EEEEEEEEEF!" came a sudden scream from the hallway. Noah came running into the cafeteria in his gym clothes. Fourth-grade lunch was at the same time as first-grade gym. "Jessica, help! A momster! The ball got away. It went into the hallway and I runned after it. And I saw it! All green and tall and ugly with those big eyes and sharp finger-nails!"

"It's *monster*, not momster," Jessica said. "And there's no such thing —"

"AHA! MAX THE MAGNIFICENT SHALL INVESTIGATE!" shouted Max, heading for the hallway. Noah raced after him.

Jessica jumped up from her seat — and stepped on a strawberry jelly doughnut. *"Bu-u-u-g!"* she shouted angrily as she slipped and slid into the hallway.

Halfway to gym, the bell rang. Lunch was over. Kids began coming out of the class-rooms left and right.

Mr. Yu, the art teacher, was in the hall-way. He was talking to the janitor, Mr. Skupa. "A school full of Russians," Mr. Skupa said. "They're always rushin'! Hee-hee-hee!"

Noah stopped at the corner of the hallway. "I saw it here. It went around the corner. It was all stiff and scary."

"Maybe you saw Mr. Skupa," Selena suggested. "He's kind of stiff and scary."

"I saw a *dinosaur*!" Noah said, marching angrily back toward the gym. "I really did!"

"I SEE THEM, TOO!" Max shouted, whirling around. "HERDS OF THEM! WE'RE UNDER ATTACK!"

"Max, those glasses have dinosaurs painted on them!" Selena said. "That's why you see so many."

"Oh," said Max.

Jessica leaned against the wall and took off her shoes. The soles were caked with strawberry jelly, so she headed for the wastebasket.

That was when she saw the long, green *thing*.

It was ripped, like paper. But it was also thick and covered with scales. She knelt down and touched it. It felt like leather or plastic. "What is *this*?"

"It looks like skin," Quincy said, kneeling next to her.

"Did dinosaurs shed their skins?" asked Max.

"It depends on the theory you believe," Quincy explained. "You see, according to the cold-blooded theory —"

"*Hey — guys? Where are you?*" Bug's voice called out from down the hallway. "*I have another trick!*"

Jessica thought of a perfect place to hide from Bug — the big janitor's closet. It had a door in back that led to the basement. Sometimes the Abracadabra Club used that door to get to their club room.

"Mr. Skupa!" she called out. "Can we hide in your closet?"

"Well, it's locked . . ." Mr. Skupa said.

What bad luck. Mr. Skupa usually left his closet open. Selena ran across the hall, to the music rooms. One door was slightly open. "Quick! In here!"

She, Selena, Max, and Quincy ran into the room and pulled the door shut. The room had no windows, so it was dark. Totally dark. A tiny bit of light came in around the edges of the door. Jessica felt along the walls for a light switch.

"Booooo," said Max.

"Stop that!" Selena said. "Jessica, this is silly. We — we can't see!"

"You are such a scaredy-cat," said Jessica.

"*Jessica?*" called Bug, from the hallway. "*Where did you go?*"

Jessica held her breath. Her eyes were

getting used to the dark now, but she still couldn't see a light switch.

She turned toward the other wall. She saw the shadow of Selena, Max, Quincy — and something else.

Something big.

Something with bulging eyes, a bald head, and pointy fingers.

4
The Magic Toilet Paper Trick

"*Let's get out of here!*" Jessica screamed. She, Quincy, Max, and Selena all tumbled out into the hallway. Kids jumped away. The door slammed shut behind them.

"Jessica, what are you doing?" Quincy asked.

"In there!" Jessica said, pointing at the music room door. "A dinosaur — or something! It had big, big eyes and pointy fingers! Didn't you guys see it?"

"I wasn't looking," said Max.

"Impossible," Quincy said, reaching for the door handle.

"NO!" yelled Selena. "Don't open that!"

Mr. Yu ran toward them. "What happened?" he called out.

"Jessica saw something in the music room," Selena said. "And I saw it, too!"

"You did?" Quincy asked.

Selena nodded. "It was just a cello. You know –– like a big violin that stands up? Somebody put a coat on it. In the dark it looked like it was alive!"

"A cello with a coat?" Jessica shook her head. She knew what a cello looked like. This wasn't a cello. It couldn't have been.

"Oh, Jessica," said Selena. "You are *such* a scaredy-cat."

One by one, everyone in the hallway began laughing.

Jessica turned and stomped away. She *hated* being laughed at.

Out of the corner of her eye, she looked for the piece of skin.

It was gone.

For the rest of the day, Jessica thought about that cello.

A cello was tall. With a coat over it, it *could* look like a creature. But what about the eyes? And the head?

When the final bell rang, she raced out of Mr. Beamish's classroom. She ran through the crowd and stopped by the music room door. When no one was looking, she pushed it wide open.

She saw trombones against the wall. A tuba, resting on a chair. A cello on its side. *No dinosaur*, she said to herself. *Must have been my imagination.*

"Jessica, will you stop chasing after monsters?" Quincy said, racing by her. "Come on! Bug Jones is heading to the club room!"

Jessica let the door slam. She rushed through the hall with Quincy, and then down the stairs to the basement.

The Abracadabra Club met in their own room in the basement, after school every Monday and Thursday. Selena and Max were already at the meeting. So was Mr. Beamish. They were all watching Bug.

"WATCH AS I, BUG THE BRILLIANT, DO THE MAGIC TOILET PAPER TRICK!" said Bug, unwrapping a roll of toilet paper.

"Wait!" Jessica yelled as she charged

into the room. "I call this meeting to order! We have lots to talk about. Quincy will begin with a report about the new job."

Jessica was the Main Brain of the Abracadabra Club — in other words, the boss. She ran all the meetings. She yelled at people who goofed off.

Jessica liked everything Perfect and Exactly the Way She Wanted It.

"'Abracadabra Club Journal, time 8:34 A.M., Monday,'" Quincy began, reading from his notepad. Quincy was the Club Scribe, or Secretary. He liked to write things down. He kept four separate books for the club. One was the Journal, for all club news and reports. Another was the Abracadabra Files, a list of all the magic tricks and how to do them. The third was the Clues Book for each mystery. And the last was the Official

Mystery Log, to record each mystery after it was solved.

"'At that time,'" Quincy read on, "'Mr. Beamish gets a phone call from Mr. Crump, Charlene's grandfather, also owner of Crump's Playworld. He is planning a big party for all of Rebus. Crump's was opened seventy-five years ago by *his* grandfather, Mr. Rufus Crump, who lived on Chestnut Street —'"

"Tell us about the *show*, Quincy!" said Selena. "The important stuff. Like, what color are the curtains — pink, red, green? Our costumes *have* to match."

Max waved his wand. "MAX THE MAGNIFICENT WILL NOT WEAR A PINK CAPE!"

Selena was the Club Designer. She was in charge of making everything look good — costumes, scenery, props, and sound. Max was the club Numa. Nobody knew exactly what that meant. But somehow it fit Max.

"We won't have much time to perform," Quincy said, still reading from his notes. "Only ten to fifteen minutes."

"Okay, let's plan five good tricks," Jessica said, "and we'll list three more, in case we need them . . ."

Mr. Beamish clasped his hands together happily. "I have been building a magic cabinet, seven feet tall, for a special disappearing trick. You wrap up someone like a mummy and put him inside. Then you close the door and —"

Bug jumped to his feet and began tearing up a long sheet of toilet paper. "I know! I can do trick number one! Watch as I rip up this paper into tiny pieces — and then make them come together again! PRESTO CHANGE-O!"

He spun around. The pieces of toilet paper flew out of his hand.

They landed smack in Selena's face.

"EWWW! P-TAAACH! P-TOOEY!" Selena ran to the sink, spitting out white bits of paper.

"Oops," Bug said, staring at the roll of toilet paper. "I'll have it ready for the show. I promise."

5

Flingosaurus

"Bug *can't* be in our show," Jessica said to Quincy on the way to school the next morning.

"Bug, bug, squash the bug," said Noah, through the helmet of his plastic knight costume.

"The Abracadabra Club is a school group," Quincy replied. "We have to be open to all students. So if Bug is in the club, he's in the show."

"Over my dead body!" said Jessica.

"*Zzzzzap!*" Noah jumped in front of her, holding out his gray plastic sword. "Your wish is my command! You're a dead body. Fall down!"

Jessica sighed and kept walking. "Why are you wearing that dumb thing?"

"To protect me from dinosaurs," Noah said, "and Carrot-heads!"

That did it. Jessica hated hated *hated* that nickname. She reached forward to grab him.

"Carrot-head! Carrot-head!" Noah ran across the school lawn, giggling.

As Noah passed a parked school bus, Andrew Flingus jumped out. He was carrying a big, inflated dinosaur, almost as tall as he was. "Nyah-hah-hah!" he said. "I am

Flingosaurus . . . and I will take over the world and eat all the little first-grade boys!"

Noah spun around and lifted his sword. "You poopy-head!" he cried, whacking the dinosaur out of Andrew's hand.

"YEEEEOW!" Andrew cried out.

The inflated dinosaur rolled onto the grass. It nearly knocked over Quincy, who was busy writing in his notepad.

"That's it!" Noah cried out. "That's the big momster I saw in the hallway yesterday!"

Jessica went closer. The dinosaur was Andrew's, so it was covered with food stains. It had green, scaly skin. Part of the skin was ripped, showing the green rubber underneath. She felt it between her fingers. It reminded her of the skin they had found in the hallway. Was this more rubbery? She wasn't sure.

"Andrew must have brought this dinosaur to school yesterday," she said. "That's what scared Noah. And then, when we ran into the hallway, he hid it — in the music room! So I didn't see a cello after all!"

"One problem," Quincy said. "Wasn't Andrew in the cafeteria the whole time?"

"Hey, get your hands off that!" Andrew shouted, running toward them.

"Andrew, can we ask you something?" Selena said.

Andrew picked up the dinosaur. He turned to Selena and burped. Then he ran toward the school.

At that moment, Max stepped off the bus. "LADIES AND GENTLEMEN . . ."

Jessica grabbed him by the arm. "Come on!"

Andrew ran through a side entrance. Jessica, Max, Quincy, and Selena followed.

But they lost him almost right away, in the back hallway of the school.

Quincy paced back and forth. "If you were Andrew, and you ran into the school to hide, where would you go?"

"The cafeteria!" said Max. "That's his favorite place."

"No, it's his *second* favorite," Jessica said, walking down the hall. "He spends much more time *there*."

She pointed to the boys' room.

Quincy looked at Max. Max looked at Quincy. "We'll handle this," said Max.

They both rolled up their sleeves and went inside.

The room wasn't very big, and Andrew was not at the sink. Quincy checked the windows to see if Andrew might have climbed out, but they were locked tight.

"Andrew?" Max called out, knocking on the stall doors.

He stopped at the last stall. He could see a pair of feet underneath. He knelt slowly for a better look.

And he froze.

The feet were bare, scaly, and green. With long, sharp claws.

"RUN!" yelled Max.

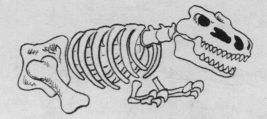

6

Stalled

"Will you guys be quiet?" Selena said, marching toward the cafeteria with Jessica. "All day long that's all you talk about — feet, feet, feet. You saw Andrew's inflated dinosaur, that's all."

"Balloon feet do not have long, pointy claws," said Quincy.

"Or scales," Max added.

Selena spun around. "*Please*, it's lunchtime! I would like to keep my appetite."

"I looked up dinosaur foot structure," Quincy said, opening his notepad. "The shape of the feet we saw was exactly correct for a two-footed dinosaur of the late Cretaceous Era."

"So now you believe there was a real dinosaur *in the boys' room*?" Jessica asked.

"I am just collecting clues," Quincy replied. "First, Noah saw something in the hallway. Then you saw it in the music room. And now Max and I saw it in the bathroom. Now, are *all* of them Andrew's dinosaur? Has Andrew been hiding that thing in the school for two days without anyone knowing about it?"

Jessica shook her head. "Andrew's not *that* smart."

"OUT OF MY WAY!" shouted Andrew, who was running toward them at top speed. "I HAVE TO GO!"

Everyone jumped out of the way. Andrew sped around the corner, nearly knocking over three second graders.

"Follow him!" Max said.

With a huge sigh, Andrew went into the boys' room.

Max stopped just short of the door.

"Well, what are you waiting for?" asked Selena.

Max gulped. "What if that *thing* is still in there?"

Quincy opened his notepad. "Let's discuss our choices here."

"Just *go*!" Jessica said.

Behind them, kids were running into the cafeteria. The hallway was quieting down.

BUMP! THWONK! came a noise from the boys' room.

Quincy dropped his notepad. Max reached into his cape for his magic wand. Selena and Jessica stood back.

Slowly the bathroom door creaked open — and Andrew appeared.

His face was white as bone, and his eyes were open wide. He stared past Max as if he wasn't there.

"Andrew?" Jessica said. "Are you all right?"

Andrew's mouth moved, but no words came out.

Then, from behind the door, a hand reached over Andrew's head. A green hand with long claws.

"*Watch out, Andrew!*" Selena shouted.

The hand grabbed Andrew's hair. It

pulled him inside the boys' room, and he let out a fearful scream.

Jessica and Selena charged the door. They pushed it open and ran into the room.

Quincy followed, holding his notepad like a shield.

"ABRACADABRA . . . MONSTRUM . . . SCRAMMO!" chanted Max, waving his magic wand as he went in last. "Wait — I think that's the right spell . . ."

Andrew was lying on the floor. He was totally still, his eyes closed.

"Is he dead?" Selena said.

Jessica knelt down to listen to his heart beat.

Brrrrrup! burped Andrew.

Jessica sprang to her feet. "Andrew, you are such a creep!"

In the corner of the bathroom, the hand

lay on the floor. It was green and scaly. "Where did you get this?" Selena asked, picking it up.

Andrew sat up and pointed at Jessica and Selena. "OOOOHHH! HEY, *TEEEEEA-*CHER! THERE ARE TWO GIRLS IN THE BOYS' BATHROOM! HAR! HAR! HAR!"

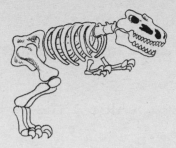

7

Reptiles Everywhere!

Jessica raced out of the boys' room. "Andrew Flingus, that was awful and sneaky and horrible and gross!"

"You forgot 'disgusting'!" said Andrew, standing in the door.

"IT WORKED! IT WORKED!" sang Max as he skipped past Andrew. "MAX THE MAGNIFICENT'S SPELL MADE THE MONSTER DISAPPEAR!"

"It wasn't a monster, Max," said Jessica. "Andrew used a fake dinosaur hand. Show him, Andrew."

"I flushed it down the toilet," Andrew replied.

"I'll find it!" Quincy declared, pushing the door open.

Selena came out of the bathroom, pulling her brush from her backpack. "Ew! My hair has boys' room smell in it — and it's your fault, Andrew!"

"Wait till I tell the principal you were in there," Andrew said, as he turned to go to the cafeteria. "And if he doesn't believe me, I'll just say, 'Smell her hair!' HAR! HAR! HAR!" Laughing, he ran to the cafeteria.

"Don't you dare," Selena called after him. "Or I'll tell him you stole that dinosaur hand!"

Quincy came out of the bathroom. "The hand is missing!"

"Who cares?" said Selena, angrily brushing her hair.

"A pair of feet . . . a hand . . ." Quincy said, pacing back and forth. "Maybe Andrew has a full dinosaur costume. He brings it to school, but it's in pieces. When no one's looking, he puts it on to scare people. That's what Noah saw in the hallway. It's what Jessica saw in the music room."

"That's the silliest thing I ever heard," Jessica said.

"I don't know about you," said Selena, walking toward the cafeteria. "But I'd rather eat than talk about disgusting boys."

Erica Landers, the snobbiest girl in fourth grade, was waiting just inside the door. "I hope you're happy, Selena Cruz," she said.

"Charlene won't come to school. She thinks she sees dinosaurs in the hallway. It's because of your dumb story in the hotel room. You hypnotized her, didn't you?"

"*What?*" Selena said.

"You and your stupid Abracadabra Club magic," Erica went on. "You got Bruce Minsky and Diane Welch, too. All three of them saw it at the same time, just before school started — a big green dinosaur."

Quincy took out his notepad and began to write. "Do you know what *kind* of dinosaur? Was it carnivorous or herbivorous? Raptor or long-necked? Cretaceous Era or Jurassic?"

"How should I know?" Erica said. "And don't stare at me. *Help! Mr. Snodgrass! The Abracadabra Club is trying to hypnotize me!*"

Jessica felt numb. Now five people had seen the dinosaur — Noah, Charlene, Bruce,

Diane, and herself. Maybe even Max and Quincy.

They couldn't all be dreaming.

Jessica, Selena, Quincy, and Max sat together. But they couldn't talk about the dinosaur problem. Just as they started to eat, Bug Jones sat down at their table.

"Go away, Bug," Jessica said.

"For today's trick, I shall turn an ordinary pack of sugar into . . . a candy bar!" Bug said, cupping his left hand. With his right hand, he shoved the sugar packet deep inside. *"Abracadabra!"*

Sugar spilled out the bottom of his fist and onto Quincy's lap.

"Yeeps!" screamed Quincy.

He leaped up from the table. His tray went the other direction, knocking into Max's tray. Both slid over the edge of the table and landed with a crash.

Everyone jumped back. Quincy tripped over Bug, who grabbed onto a pile of backpacks at the edge of the table.

Trays, backpacks, Quincy, and Bug hit the floor together.

"Children, please!" shouted Mr. Snodgrass, the teacher on lunch duty. "Will someone get some napkins?"

"There's juice in my hair!" screamed Selena, brushing it out as fast as she could.

"HAR! HAR! HAR!" laughed Andrew from the next table.

Selena and Max picked up books that had fallen in juice. Jessica got some napkins. She and Bug began wiping the table.

But below the table, Quincy was still. His eyes were on something that had dropped onto the floor. Something he had not expected to see.

A scaly, green dinosaur hand.

8

Questioning Quincy

Jessica's footsteps sounded hollow in the hallway. School was over, and everyone had gone home.

Everyone except her, Max, Selena, and Quincy.

"What does Quincy want?" whispered Selena.

"I don't know," Max replied. "He just said to meet him at the library."

"He's been acting weird ever since that mess in the cafeteria yesterday," said Selena.

"Well, he better get over it," Jessica said. "We have a huge show on Saturday!"

Mrs. Wegman, the librarian, waved to them from the front desk. Then she pointed to a corner by the window.

There, behind a table piled high with books, sat Quincy. He was busy writing in his notepad.

As Jessica got closer, she looked over his shoulder to see what he was doing:

"You can *draw*?" Max asked.

Quincy shut his notepad, put it in his backpack, and stood up. "Follow me," he said.

"Quincy, what's going on?" asked Selena as they walked away from the library.

"You'll see." Quincy headed down one hallway, then another. He walked through

the lobby, and then down another hallway. Mr. Skupa, the janitor, was mopping the floor and singing an old song. "Watch your step!" he called out.

Just past Mr. Skupa, Quincy turned right, then stopped. Two doors down, the art room was open.

"Yesterday in the cafeteria," whispered Quincy, "I saw a piece of evidence."

"Why didn't you tell us?" asked Jessica.

"I couldn't," Quincy said. "I had to be very careful. Because I believe that a member of the Abracadabra Club is involved in this mystery."

"Impossible!" said Max.

"The Abracadabra Club does not keep secrets!" Jessica said.

Selena shook her head. "Quincy, this makes no sense."

"Perhaps," said Quincy, turning to walk down the hall. "Let's find out. Come with me — and please, just agree with everything I say."

In the art room, Mr. Yu was busy tidying up. He looked surprised when the four kids walked in.

"Hi, we're doing a project for Mr. Beamish," Quincy said, opening his notepad on Mr. Yu's desk. "He wants us to draw a realistic *Triceratops*. We have to do it from memory — from what we saw in New York. Right, guys?"

"Uh, right!" Max replied.

"We're working on it together," Jessica added.

"Right!" Max piped up.

Mr. Yu looked carefully at Quincy's drawing. His face got very serious. "Well,

I'm sorry to say, but that's not a *Triceratops*, Quincy."

"Oh, no," said Quincy, "I must have gotten mixed up. It looks like *one* of the dinosaurs we saw. I forget which . . ."

"WOW! Quincy actually *forgot* something?" Max said.

Jessica elbowed him in the side.

"I mean . . . *right*!" Max squeaked.

"It's walking on two legs . . . it has a long neck . . . its claws have a kind of thumb," Mr. Yu said, nodding. "The angle of the snout, the size of the brain area . . . This is amazing, Quincy. You have a perfect memory — you just got the dinosaur name wrong. This is exactly like a *Stenonychosaurus*."

A big smile spread slowly across Quincy's face. He slammed his notebook shut and headed for the door. "Okay, thanks! 'Bye! Come on, guys, let's go!"

Quincy ran down the hallway. "Guys, there really is a dinosaur in the school." As they turned the corner, he called out, "Mr. Skupa! Please open the janitor's closet!"

Mr. Skupa looked up. "My closet? Why, it's locked."

"That's funny, you never used to lock it before," Quincy said, walking straight for the closet. "You always let us go through, to get to the back stairs. Let's see what's inside."

"Well, uh . . ." Mr. Skupa said, scratching his head.

"No!" Selena blurted out.

Jessica was confused and scared. What was going on?

From behind them, Mr. Yu's voice rang

out: "It's okay, Selena. Go ahead, Mr. Skupa. Open the door."

"If you say so," said Mr. Skupa with a shrug.

He inserted the key and pulled open the door.

At that moment, loud footsteps sounded from around the corner. "HEY, GUYS! LOOK!"

Bug Jones came racing into the hallway, holding a deck of cards. He smashed into the open door. His cards went flying, and he tumbled to the floor. He landed facing the Abracadabra Club. "Oops . . ."

But no one noticed. They were all staring at what was in the closet.

"Guys?" Bug said.

Slowly, he turned around. He saw what was in Mr. Skupa's closet.

And he screamed.

9

Stage Fright

"Ladies and gentlemen!" Mayor Kugel's voice rang out over the parking lot. "We are very proud to celebrate the seventy-fifth birthday of Rebus' very own amusement park, Crump's Playworld. We have quite a show for you today!"

The Abracadabra Club sat on a wide stage. Behind them, the Ferris wheel cast a big shadow. The parking lot was full of people in folding chairs — hundreds of them.

It was chilly outside. Jessica was so excited she could hardly sit. The mystery had been solved and the show had a great new trick.

"Pssst," Selena whispered. "What if it scares everybody?"

"It's like nothing anyone has ever seen before," said Quincy.

"If they all scream and run away," Max asked, "will they arrest us?"

"And now, to start things out," Mayor Kugel said, "the Abracadabra Club of Rebus Elementary School!"

As the crowd cheered, Jessica looked out and saw her mom and dad waving from the front row. Noah was sticking out his tongue.

Max was supposed to open the show. But

he was shaking. "I — I'm scared," he said. "And I forgot the spell for curing stage fright!"

"Just go!" Selena urged, pushing him toward the front of the stage.

"UM . . . WELCOME ALL YOU REBUS CINNAMONS!" Max shouted.

"It's *citizens*, not *cinnamons*!" Jessica said in a loud whisper.

Max whooshed his cape as he walked to the center of the stage, "TO START OUR SHOW, I, MAX THE MAGNIFICENT, SHALL —"

But before Max could finish, Bug Jones came running down the center aisle. "Sorry! Sorry, I'm late!"

Jessica couldn't believe it. *"Not now, Bug!"*

Bug hopped up on the stage, right in front of Max. In his hand was a roll of toilet paper. "Hi, everybody! This is the coolest trick! See, I take this long sheet of toilet paper, and I rip it into pieces . . ."

"UH, LIKE I SAID," Max went on, "I, MAX THE MAGNIFICENT, SHALL —"

"Psssst!" From backstage, Mr. Beamish waved to Max. He was holding something blue and round in his hand. It looked like a little water balloon.

"And now — *abracadabra* — the pieces will come together!" Bug said. He opened his hand and teeny shreds of toilet paper fell to the floor. "Oops! Uh, wait —"

Max took the roll of toilet paper out of Bug's hand. "WHAT HE MEANS IS . . . THIS!" He ripped up another long sheet, then stuffed the pieces into the palm of his hand. "ABRACADABRA!" he shouted, unrolling one long sheet from his palm. It was as though the ripped pieces of toilet paper had magically come back together.

This time, the crowd clapped.

"Give me that!" said Bug, grabbing the sheet of toilet paper.

Max did not let go — and suddenly, water began squirting out of the toilet paper, right into Bug's face.

"Hey — wha —glurb!" Bug shouted.

Max bowed, then gave the mike to Selena.

She stood in front of the magic cabinet that Mr. Beamish had built. She and Mr. Beamish were holding a long, long, white sheet. "Looks like our friend needs to dry off," said Selena. "Let's give him this!"

She and Max patted Bug's face with the sheet. "Now, just follow along," Jessica whispered into Bug's ear. "This is the best trick of all!"

They began wrapping him in the sheet — and wrapping — and wrapping. The sheet was long enough to wrap Bug like a mummy.

Gently, they pushed him into the magic cabinet. "A few seconds in our drying machine, and he'll be like new!" Selena said.

They closed the door. Together they turned the cabinet around.

"ABRACADABRA!" they all shouted at once.

From below the stage, Mr. Beamish used a special machine to make a flash of smoke. Jessica turned the cabinet around one last time.

Then she pulled the door open.

An outline appeared through the smoke. Two bulging eyes. A long, green body. Hands with thin, pointy fingers.

The whole audience gasped.

Slowly, the creature raised its right arm. "Be not afraid," it called out. "My name is Stan."

10

Stan

"Fantastic!" shouted Mayor Kugel, shaking Mr. Beamish's hand. "Your club was the hit of the show! Not to mention the — the —"

"*Stenonychosaurus* model," Quincy said. "With moving parts. But you can call him Stan."

The show was finally over. Everyone had gathered near the stage. The Cruz, Norton,

Frimmel, and Bleeker families were all taking pictures of one another.

But most everybody was lining up to meet Stan. "THANK YOU, THANK YOU!" shouted Max. "LET'S KEEP IT MOVING, FOLKS! STEP RIGHT UP AND MAX THE MAGNIFICENT WILL INTRODUCE YOU TO THE FAMOUS STAN, THE MARVEL OF POLLUTION!"

"*Evolution!*" Quincy corrected him.

Mr. Beamish felt the "skin" of the *Stenonychosaurus* model. "He seems so real!"

"Thank you," said Mr. Yu. "I started working on him months ago, when I first read about the American Museum of Natural History's contest. It seemed like a great idea — imagining a dinosaur evolved into the twenty-first century. I always did want to make models for a museum. So I decided to enter — but I wanted to keep it a secret until I was done. I told only Mr. Skupa, because I needed his closet to store the model. Then one day, after school, while I was working on Stan's head, there was a knock on my door — it was Selena!"

"He tried to hide the model, but I kept asking questions," Selena said. "Finally, he told me the truth. And he let me be his assistant — as long as I kept the secret."

"So *that's* why you were being so sneaky," Jessica said. "It was Mr. Yu's fault."

"Everything was going fine," said Selena. "Until nosy Andrew started taking things — stuff that Mr. Yu had given me to work on. Like Stan's hand . . ."

"That's what we saw in the boys' room!" Max exclaimed.

"Precisely," said Quincy.

"How did you figure all this out, Quincy?" asked Selena.

"Simple," Quincy replied. "When we went back into the bathroom, the hand was gone. Which meant someone had taken it. At first I thought Andrew had it. But when Bug made that big mess in the cafeteria, I saw the dinosaur hand — right next to Selena's wide-open backpack! Well, I couldn't figure out why Selena would have it. But then I remembered she had accused Andrew of *stealing* the hand. I wondered how she *knew* it was stolen. Stolen from whom? Who would own a perfect model *Stenonychosaurus* hand? Or a set of perfect *Stenonychosaurus* feet?"

"Someone making a perfect *Stenony-chosaurus* model!" Jessica piped up.

"Exactly!" said Quincy. "Which meant we were looking for a scientist or an artist.

Ms. Mandible, the museum lady, told us she had put ads in the art magazines. Well, Mr. Yu's room is filled with art magazines. Plus, remember how he admired the stuffed dinosaur models at the museum? He was looking at them all so closely. It made sense that he would enter the contest — and that his best student, Selena, might be helping him. Then I thought about Mr. Skupa and his locked closet — and I put two and two together."

"Four!" Max exclaimed brightly.

"The closet was a perfect place to hide a dinosaur model," Quincy said. "But I still wasn't sure. So, as a test, I drew a perfect *Stenonychosaurus*, showed it to Mr. Yu, and pretended it was something else. When he recognized the Steno — and knew so much about it — I knew I was right. Mystery solved!"

"But what about all those dinosaur sightings?" Jessica asked. "And the skin we found on the floor? And the feet Max and Quincy saw?"

Mr. Yu laughed. "I've been coming into school at night to work on Stan. I would come in before the morning bell rings. I'd work during lunch. Sometimes I'd get so carried away, I'd lose track of time. Then I would have to drag Stan into the closet at the last minute, so no one would see him. One time I was in such a hurry, I pulled Stan against the trophy case, and he ripped. A few other times, I couldn't even get to the closet in time. I'd have to hide him wherever I could."

"The music room," Jessica said.

"The boys' room," Max added.

"I wish I had been more careful," Mr. Yu admitted.

"Me, too," Jessica said. "Poor Noah. He's so scared, I don't think he'll ever get over it."

"Well, good luck," Mr. Beamish said. "I hope you win the contest."

Mr. Yu smiled. "Thanks. If I win a trophy, I'll make sure Selena's name is on it."

"Cool!" said Selena.

"Wheeeee!" came Noah's voice from behind them.

Andrew Flingus was holding him off the ground. Noah had one arm on Stan's shoulder, another on Stan's wrist. "Look, Jessica, we're dancing!"

"HAR! HAR! HAR!" laughed Andrew. Jessica smiled.

Noah was going to be just fine.

And so was Stan.

The Abracadabra Files by Quincy
Magic Trick #18
The "Pick-a-fruit" Trick

Ingredients:
1 shopping bag
Several pieces of fruit
1 piece of paper
1 pen or pencil
1 hat

How I Did It:

1. I asked everyone to pick the name of a fruit. As each person called out a name, I wrote something down on a piece of paper. Then I put each paper in Max's hat.
2. After everyone was finished, I asked Andrew to pick a piece of paper from the hat. I told him to keep the name of the fruit a secret. Then I pulled a banana out of the hat — which was the name on the piece of paper Andrew had chosen!
3. The trick? Back in step 1, as everyone

was calling out the name of a fruit, I
wrote "banana" on each sheet — every
single one! They couldn't see what I
was writing, so they <u>thought</u> I was
writing down all the different names.
So no matter what sheet I picked, it
was the right answer!

The Abracadabra Files by Quincy
Magic Trick #19

The Old Hand Behind the Door Trick
(This Is the Oldest Trick in the Book.)

Ingredients:
1 open door
1 hand (Andrew used the dinosaur hand, but your own will do.)

How Andrew Did It:

1. He stood against the side of the door, so his right arm was hidden.
2. He reached over his own head, holding the dinosaur hand!

BOYS' ROOM

The Abracadabra Files by Quincy
Magic Trick #20
Ripped Toilet Paper Comes
Together Again

Ingredients:
1 roll of toilet paper

How Max Did It (and Bug Didn't):

1. Before starting, he cupped the fingers
    of his left hand. Then he rolled up a wad
    of toilet paper and
    tucked it in his
    fingers.
2. He ripped up a
    length of toilet
    paper in front of the
    crowd. Then he mushed it all together.
    Secretly, he switched the hidden
    ball of toilet paper with
    the ripped-up one.
3. Then he unfolded the
    hidden ball, which was
    still in one piece!

The Abracadabra Files by Quincy
Magic Trick #21
The Squirting Toilet Paper

Ingredients:
1 large party balloon
1 pin
1/4 cup of water
1 wad of toilet paper

How Max Did It:

1. He prepared before the show. He took one large balloon and poured about 1/4 cup of water into it. It was a big balloon, so it stayed limp.
2. With a pin, he poked eight holes into the balloon (which was very hard to do!). Because there was so little air in the balloon, it didn't leak. Max gave the balloon to Mr. Beamish to hold until Max needed it.
3. When Bug tried to grab the wad of toilet paper from Max, Max took the balloon Mr. Beamish had handed him. He placed it inside the toilet paper — and squeezed!

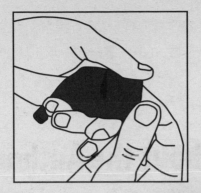

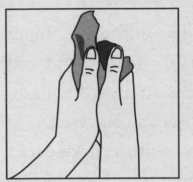

About the Author

Peter Lerangis is the author of many different kinds of books for readers of many ages, including *Watchers*, an award-winning science-fiction/mystery series; *Antarctica*, a two-book exploration adventure; and several hilarious novels for young children, including *Spring Fever!*, *Spring Break*, *It Came from the Cafeteria*, and *Attack of the Killer Potatoes*. His recent movie adaptations include *The Sixth Sense* and *Like Mike*. He lives in New York City with his wife, Tina deVaron, and their two sons, Nick and Joe.